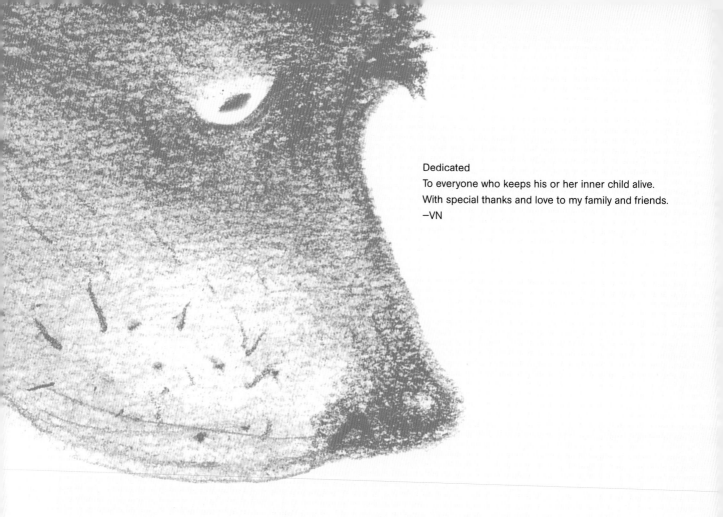

Dedicated
To everyone who keeps his or her inner child alive.
With special thanks and love to my family and friends.
—VN

Published in 2015 by Simply Read Books www.simplyreadbooks.com

Text & Illustrations © 2015 Vanya Nastanlieva

Library and Archives Canada Cataloguing in Publication

Nastanlieva, Vanya, author, illustrator
     Mo and Beau / written and illustrated by Vanya Nastanlieva.

ISBN 978-1-927018-63-7 (bound)

I. Title.
PZ7.N375Mo 2015   j823'.92   C2014-905983-3

We gratefully acknowledge for their financial support of our publishing program the Canada Council for the Arts, the BC Arts Council, and the Government of Canada through the Canada Book Fund (CBF).

Manufactured in Malaysia
Book design by hundreds & thousands

10 9 8 7 6 5 4 3 2 1

Vanya Nastanlieva

MO and BEAU

Simply Read Books

Little Mo wanted to play.

So he found **big Beau**.

Tweak, tweak...

Beau opened his eyes.

Mo opened his eyes.

Beau showed off his teeth.

Mo showed off his teeth.

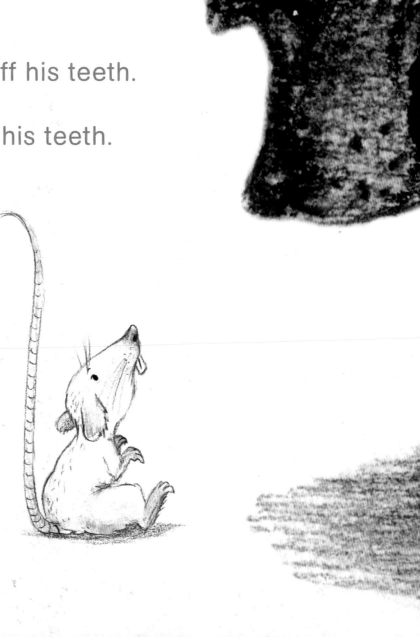

Beau took a long, deep breath of air.

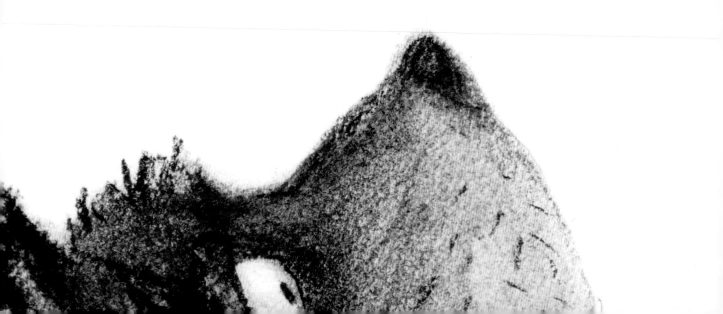

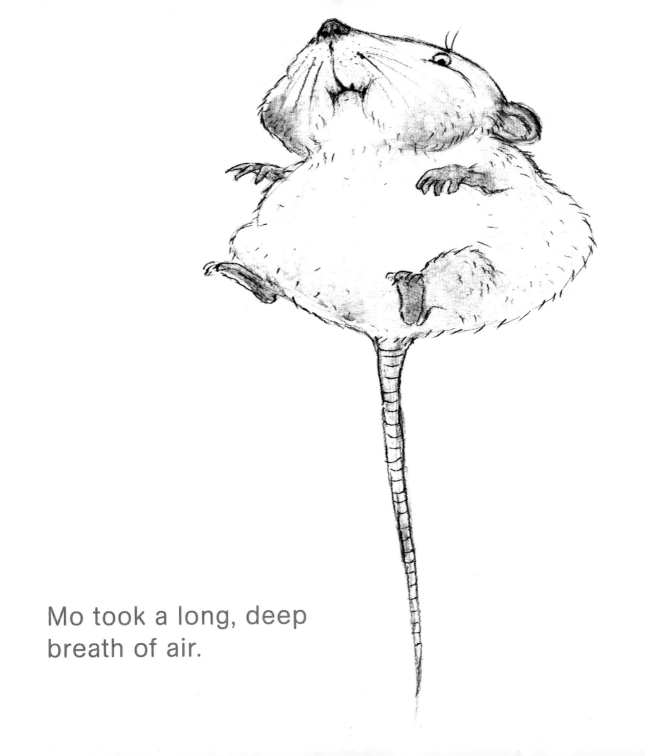

Mo took a long, deep
breath of air.

Beau

ROARED.

Mo squeaked.

Beau bristled his fur.

Mo bristled his fur.

Beau stretched.

Mo stretched.

Beau scratched himself.

Mo scratched himself.

Beau gave a **BIG** yawn.

Mo gave a **BIG** yawn.

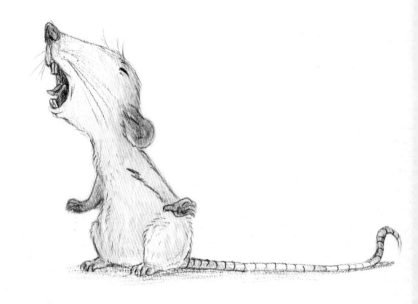

Beau fell asleep.

But what about Mo?

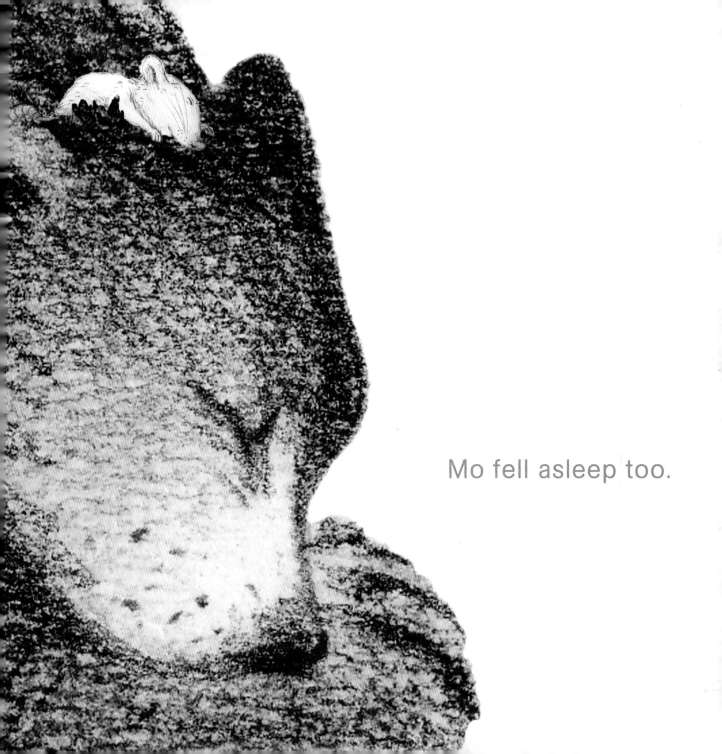

Mo fell asleep too.

But not for long…